Monkey
Monster
Truck

ISBN 978-0-9846528-1-5

Printed in the U.S.A.

First Printing, March 2012

Monkey See, Monkey Do.

Monkey Puts You in the Zoo!

CONTENTS

Real Heroes Read!

#13: Monkey Monster Truck

David Anthony
and
Charles David Clasman

Illustrations
Lys Blakeslee

Traverse City, MI

Home of the Heroes

abigail

zoë

andrew

CHAPTER 1:
MEET THE HEROES

Welcome to Traverse City, Michigan, population 18,000. The city has everything you might expect: malls, movie theaters, schools, and playgrounds. Kids swim here in the summer and build snowmen during the winter. Sometimes they pretend that they live in an ordinary place.

But Traverse City is far from ordinary. It is set on one of the Great Lakes and attracts tourists in every season. Thousands of people visit every year.

Still, few of them know the city's real secret. Even fewer talk about it. You see, Traverse City is home to three marvelous superheroes. This story is about them.

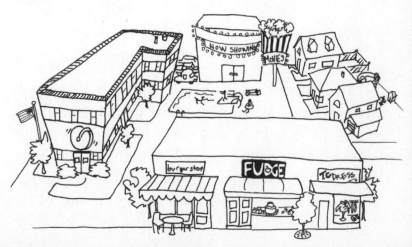

Meet Abigail, the oldest of our heroes by a whole eight minutes. When it comes to sports, she can't be beat—not at martial arts, not at mountain climbing, and certainly not at running marathons. She's the MVP of every sport—the most valuable player. Abigail could even out-climb King Kong up the side of the Empire State Building in New York City.

Andrew comes next. He's Abigail's twin brother, younger by a measly eight minutes. If it has wheels, Andrew can ride it. He's masterful, magnificent, and the man on wheels. Not even the proverbial barrel of monkeys would give him trouble. He could chariot those chimps straight to the zoo.

Last but definitely not least is Baby Zoë. She's proof that big things can come in small packages. She still wears a diaper, but she can fly to the moon and back faster than you can say Swiss cheese. What's that? The Space Shuttle needs help? Zoë to the rescue. She puts the *miss* in *mission*.

Together these three heroes keep the streets and neighborhoods of Traverse City, Michigan, and America safe. Together they are …

CHAPTER 2:
CRIME CRUSHER

"Muscles," Zoë said, stating the obvious. Nearby, her brother and sister shared a look. *There she goes again.*

"That's right, Zoë," Abigail said patiently. "You have super strength."

"You sure do," Andrew agreed. "We couldn't have built this truck without you."

Zoë nodded enthusiastically. She was proud of herself. It wasn't every baby sister that could lift a truck over her head. What better way for her brother to give it an oil change?

Dad strolled out of the house. "You kids need any help?" he offered. "I was pretty handy in auto shop class back in high school. I had a regular green thumb."

The twins shot him a look.

"A green thumb?" Abigail inquired.

"That's for plants, not cars and trucks," Andrew said, rolling his eyes.

Dad chuckled. "Shows what you know. My assignment was to restore an old 1949 Cadillac Fleetwood. Wood and wheels takes a green thumb."

Fortunately the heroes' truck was nothing like Dad's ancient wreck. They named the vehicle *Crime Crusher* and it looked ready to do exactly that. Crush crime and anything else in its way.

A red, white, and blue paint job gave the truck a patriotic presence. Wheels as tall as tigers made it seem like a crouching cat, preparing to pounce. Police sirens crowned its roof. There was no doubt this vehicle raced for the good guys.

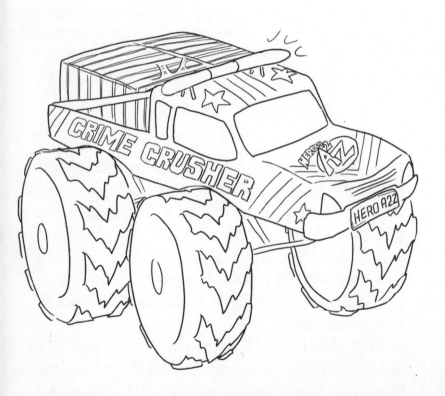

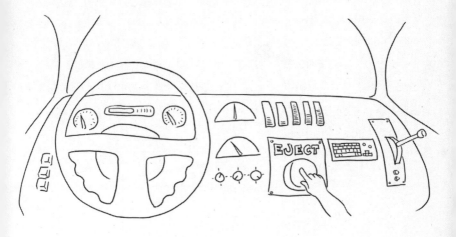

Crime Crusher could even fly. Zoë had insisted upon that. No vehicle of hers would be stuck on the ground any more than she was. So the heroes had fitted *Crime Crusher* with a special feature: an eject button.

Pushing *Crime Crusher's* eject button caused something amazing to happen. No, it didn't blast the passengers from their seats. That was for jets and other normal aircraft. Pushing eject blasted *Crime Crusher* into the air—the whole truck, passengers included. Rocket blasters sent it skyward. Then its titanic tires swelled, filling with helium.

The heroes believed in being prepared. Especially because they had signed up for Michigan Monster Truck Mayhem, also called M2TM. The monster truck event combined freestyle competition with timed racing. If the heroes wanted to win, they and their truck needed to be ready for anything.

CHAPTER 3:
MEET THE MONSTER TRUCKS

"Messy," Zoë said, peering out the car's window.

She and her family had just pulled into the parking lot of the Berlin Raceway, home of M2TM. They pulled *Crime Crusher* on a trailer behind them. The raceway was located in Marne, Michigan, on the western side of the state in the Lower Peninsula.

Messy described the parking lot perfectly today. Someone had tossed banana peels everywhere. Some were bright yellow, others greenish and not quite ripe. Most curled in the summer heat, turning black and rotting.

Abigail crinkled her nose. "Who would throw their garbage everywhere?" she wondered.

"A selfish slob who doesn't have to clean up," Andrew responded.

Farther into the parking lot, the banana peels disappeared. Here the heroes encountered their competition. The M2TM judges had invited eight trucks and eight drivers to the event. Andrew and *Crime Crusher* were one pair. The other seven contestants had already arrived.

First up: *Dragon Wagon* and its mysterious driver known only as the Black Knight. Both vehicle and driver were encased in metal—the driver in medieval armor, the truck in shining plates and parts.

"Mantis," Zoë hissed, when she spotted the second driver and truck.

Miami Mantis and her truck *Lady Buggy* had made the trip from Florida. As you would expect from their names, truck and driver resembled insects. They had antennas and looked as friendly as wasps. No wonder Zoë hissed.

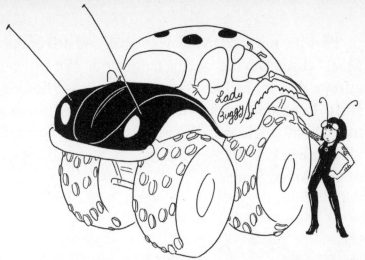

Rockness Monster hulked in the next parking spot. Built like a tank, the earth-toned monster truck resembled both a monster and a truck. If they had been carved out of solid rock, that is!

The truck's driver, Rocky Barbella, was a big man. His muscles had muscles and he never smiled. Win or lose, Mr. Barbella was as stable as stone. Where was he from? Boulder, Colorado, of course.

Pass the mustard to the next truck and driver duo. Meet Darren Deville and his unique ride *Hot Dogger,* a truck that looks like—you guessed it—a hotdog! Not to be outdone by his vehicle, Darren Deville *acted* like a hotdog. He was a fearless showoff who made his home in Las Vegas, Nevada—the showoff capital of the United States.

Lurking nearby, *Squeal Mobile* was as dark as a moonless midnight. Bottomless black paint cloaked the vehicle in shadow—bumper to bumper, and door to door.

The vehicle's driver, Robin Graves, remained a mystery to all. No one knew her age, her face, or the name of her hometown. Ms. Graves was as guarded as a ghost.

Hunter Bowman nodded as the heroes and their parents passed. He drove Michigan's own *Taxi Derby*, a favorite monster truck of outdoorsmen throughout the state. Mr. Bowman and his vehicle were covered in camouflage but also matted in mud. There wasn't a track they wouldn't attack. The pair preferred the nitty-gritty and down-to-earth.

"That's quite an assortment of trucks and drivers," Dad said as he pulled into a parking spot.

"Motley," Zoë agreed.

Splat!

Suddenly a banana peel landed wetly on the car's windshield. Startled, Dad hit the brakes harder than necessary. "Where did that come from?" he blinked.

The answer was obvious. In the spot next to the car, two massive gorillas wearing striped suits folded their arms and scowled.

The heroes stared back. They knew those gorillas. They formed the crew of the eighth and final driver. A driver who would soon drive all of them completely bananas.

CHAPTER 4:
CHAMP THE CHIMP

One of the gorillas pointed a wrinkled, meaty hand at Andrew. "Hey, look, it's Kid Stroll," it said.

Now Andrew scowled. Kid Roll was his superhero identity. Kid *Stroll* was an insult. A stroll was a slow way to travel. Nothing like Andrew on a set of wheels.

"I thought he was Skid Roll," the other ape said. "Which is what he will do today when he crashes—skid and then roll!"

Both of the gorillas laughed. Andrew hunched down in his seat, trying to ignore them.

The gorillas served as bodyguards to a very special monkey. Known as Champ the Chimp, the monkey was the top driver on the monster truck circuit. He wasn't really a chimpanzee though. Chimps were apes and didn't have tails.

In his vehicle, *Monkey Business,* Champ had never lost a race or competition. He had earned the Champ portion of his nickname in battle. He had demolished drivers and trounced trucks from Connecticut to California. Today he was looking forward to doing the same to Andrew.

4

"Ignore those apes," Mom told Andrew. "Win or lose, we will still love you. Isn't that right, everyone?"

Andrew sank lower into his seat. Mom's words were kind but not the kind of words he wanted to hear. Luckily his sisters knew what to do.

"Meathead!" Zoë zinged the first gorilla.

"Bananasaurus Pecks," Abigail accused the second.

If the over-muscled gorillas were going to talk trash, the heroes could dish out the same.

The gargantuan gorillas bellowed and beat their chests. How dare Abigail and Zoë call them names—especially names that fit!

Before the verbal war could really explode, a new voice silenced everyone. It blared from loudspeakers all over the raceway grounds.

"Attention, drivers. Please report to the starting area. This year's Michigan Monster Truck Mayhem is about to begin."

Andrew pumped a fist in the air. His sisters had beaten the gorillas with words. Now it was his turn to beat Champ the Chimp on the racetrack.

CHAPTER 5:
ROUND ONE

The announcer's voice continued to blare across the racetrack grounds. His speedy words ran together like an auctioneer's.

"Welcome, welcome, ladies and gents! Welcome, children, seniors, and everyone in between. Welcome to the 13th annual Michigan Monster Truck Mayhem!"

Excitement erupted throughout the crowd. Children cheered. Adults applauded. One frantic fan even fainted and fell down.

When the crowd noise faded, the announcer continued.

"Today's car-crunching competition will feature eight wheeled warriors. They will smash, crash, and thrash their way through three rowdy rounds and seven bruising battles. In the end, only one will emerge triumphant and wear the victor's crown."

Again the crowd hooted and howled, but the announcer continued.

"Let Round One begin!"

CRIME CRUSHER vs HOT DOGGER
ROCKNESS MONSTER vs LADY BUGGY
TAXI DERBY vs DRAGON WAGON
MONKEY BUSINESS vs SQUEAL MOBILE

Andrew swallowed nervously. Sure, he was Kid Roll, a superhero on wheels. But his competition included some of the best monster truck drivers in the country. Who wouldn't be nervous facing such odds?

"Please be careful," Mom cautioned.

"Just do you best," Dad said. "We don't care who wins."

His sisters, however, weren't as worried or supportive. Abigail stared hard into her brother's eyes. "Flatten 'em," she said about the other drivers.

"Mash!" Zoë seconded, smacking her palms together forcefully.

In the lane to Andrew's right, Darren Deville gave him a thumbs-up. Andrew smiled politely in return but also revved his engine. This was it. The first event of M2TM. *Hot Dogger* vs. *Crime Crusher* in a slap wheelie competition. The drivers could be good sportsmen now, friends later.

Three … two … one … Go!

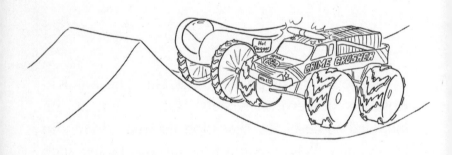

Andrew and Darren hit the gas at the same time. Their trucks rushed noisily into motion. Straight ahead of them awaited a ramp high enough and wide enough to propel them both into the air.

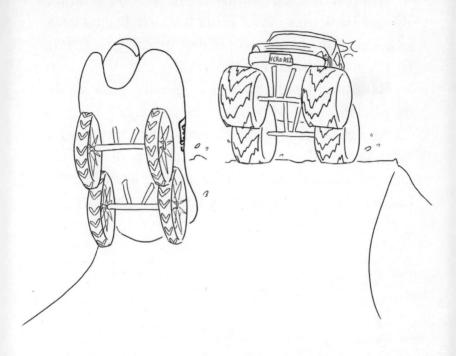

Vrooom!

Hot Dogger hit the ramp first, Andrew a split second later. Speed, though, wasn't the goal in this event. Distance after the landing won.

Wham!

Hot Dogger landed on its back tires and then slammed its front onto the track. *Slap!* The impact heaved the vehicle into an improbable wheelie. Darren Deville then gunned his accelerator and sped down the track. The nose of his truck remained in the air.

Andrew landed another split second behind. *Wham!* Back tires. *Slap!* Front tires. He leaned back in his seat and slammed his foot on the gas. *Crime Crusher* wheelied down the track.

Both trucks seemed to defy gravity. How could they balance on just two tires for so long?

Andrew, of course, didn't worry about such things. Wheelie wonders were part of his superpower. He concentrated and clenched the steering wheel in both hands. His eyes and attention never left the track.

Darren Deville, on the other hand, couldn't resist playing up to the crowd. His truck was named *Hot Dogger* for good reason. Both of them were unapologetic showoffs!

So what happened next surprised no one. Darren released his steering wheel and thrust his hands out the open driver side window. He waved comically to the audience. Look, everyone, no hands!

Wham!

He also lost control of his truck. *Hot Dogger's* front tires crashed to the track, and Andrew sped past, still pulling a wheelie.

Just like that, the event ended. Andrew won and would move on to Round Two.

Next up, *Rockness Monster* vs. *Lady Buggy*. The pair would meet in the Splash Dash. Unlike Andrew's first event, the Splash Dash depended solely on speed.

Race straight down a long, narrow track. Build up speed. Then hydroplane over a pool of water as far as possible before sinking. The first to sink lost. Plug your nose and go home.

Lady Buggy took an early lead and never looked back. The sleek truck was light and built for speed. And like many bugs, it also had wings! *Rockness Monster* didn't stand a chance. It sank quickly and exactly like—you guessed it—a rock.

Match-up three pitted *Taxi Derby* against *Dragon Wagon*. It was buck vs. beast in a distance-devouring feast. Whichever vehicle jumped the farthest won.

Bang! The starting gun fired, and the trucks peeled into motion. Side-by-side they tore down the track neck-and-neck.

Whoom-whoom! They screamed up the ramp and hurtled into the air. What height! What distance! Both shattered track records. Could these vehicles really fly?

Yes, one of them could. *Dragon Wagon*. Like a real fire-breathing dragon, flames erupted from the back of the vehicle. They propelled it on to victory and Round Two.

The final event of Round One matched *Monkey Business* vs. *Squeal Mobile*. They met in the Donut Derby, spinning 'round and 'round until one fell down.

Which didn't take long.

As soon as the trucks started spinning, Champ's helmet pulsed with energy. The monkey then tossed a banana peel onto the track, which no one else noticed.

Driver Robin Graves in *Squeal Mobile* couldn't avoid the peel. In mid-donut, she slid over the slippery skin and skidded out of control. She rolled once, twice, and crashed into a barricade.

Champ squealed to a stop, raising his arms in triumph. He and the other victors were headed to Round Two.

CHAPTER 6:
ROUND TWO

Round Two of Michigan Monster Truck Mayhem began almost immediately. This round would consist of two events. The winners would meet in the M2TM Finals next round. The losers would be sent to the garage. Win or go home, as the saying went.

MONKEY BUSINESS vs DRAGON WAGON

LADY BUGGY vs CRIME CRUSHER

"We begin Round Two with something new," the racetrack announcer rhymed. "Perhaps you've seen a drag race once. But have you seen race draggin' stunts? Behold!"

On the south end of the track, *Monkey Business* and *Dragon Wagon* revved their engines. Attached to each vehicle was a trailer loaded with surprising cargo: horses! Or, more specifically, marble sculpted into the shape of mustangs. The towering statues must have weighed tons! Much more weight than the trucks had been designed to haul.

Nevertheless, haul they did, like muscular tow trucks down the track. Their roaring engines chugged black smoke into the air. Their burning tires heaved clods of dirt onto the crowd.

It looked like the pair of vehicles would either explode from effort or cross the finish line in a dead heat, a tie. Either way, the audience would get its money's worth.

Dragon Wagon's driver, the Black Knight, refused to settle for a tie. He had lost to Champ before. Never again, he had vowed. Today he would win at any cost.

Seeing Champ so close infuriated him. So he reached for his secret weapon again: *Dragon Wagon's* flame thrusters.

Whooosh!

Fire belched from the rear of his vehicle, blasting him into the lead. Seconds later, he crossed the finish line a truck length ahead of Champ.

The winner? Champ in *Monkey Business,* of course. He finished with his cargo intact. The Black Knight had burned his to ash, trailer included. Disqualified!

As Andrew prepared for his next event, his stomach churned nervously. Champ the Chimp had won! The monkey was going to the Finals.

"I don't know if I can beat him," Andrew admitted.

"Him?" Abigail wondered. "Don't get ahead of yourself. You're up against Miami Mantis next. Stay focused."

"Meditate!" Zoë admonished. *Think, Andrew, use your head.*

Their tag team approach made Andrew feel as if he were in a wrestling match instead of a monster truck rally. No fair, two against one!

Coincidentally, Andrew met Miami Mantis in a ring. Not a square wrestling ring. An actual circle painted in the middle of the racetrack. The event? The Bumper Buster, a sumo wrestling match on wheels.

Andrew pulled *Crime Crusher* slowly into the circle. Miami Mantis did the same in *Lady Buggy*. They met in the center, facing one another. Their front bumpers touched gently, nose to nose.

"I'm going to squish you, kid," Miami Mantis sneered.

"Like a bug?" Andrew replied, guessing where this was going.

Miami Mantis's sneer deepened. "Never mind!"

Score one for Andrew.

He would need it, too. Any advantage. Because when the gun sounded, Miami Mantis buried her gas pedal. *Vrooom! Lady Buggy* lurched forward like an angry bull released from a pen.

Andrew fought back, slamming down his own pedal. For a moment, *Lady Buggy* shoved him backward. Then *Crime Crusher* responded and the vehicles muscled into a stalemate. Neither gave ground, forward or back. Yet the first to push the other out of the ring would win.

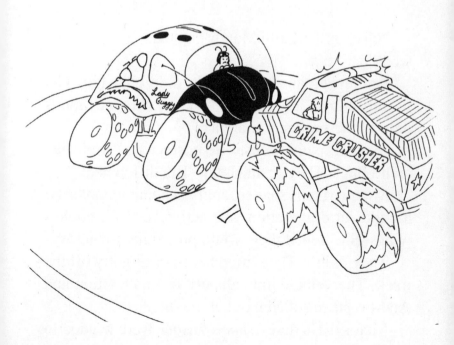

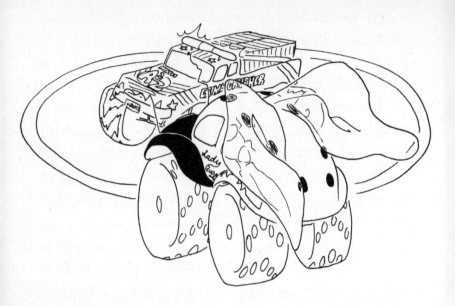

"Give up!" Miami Mantis taunted. "You're in my web!"

Andrew groaned. The insults didn't bug him. Get it? *Bug* him. Lady *Buggy*. Anyway, Miami Mantis didn't have her facts straight.

"Spiders spin webs," he corrected. "And they aren't bugs. They're arachnids. Big difference!"

Miami Mantis snarled, angry at being schooled by a child. In desperation, she activated her vehicle's wings. She hoped they would propel her to victory.

They didn't. They lifted her truck slightly off the track. The vehicle immediately lost its traction and Andrew steamrolled it out of the ring.

Victory! He and *Crime Crusher* were headed to the Finals!

CHAPTER 7:
THUMBS-UP/THUMBS-DOWN

M2TM hosted a question and answer session with the remaining drivers before the Finals. Andrew and Champ were invited onto a round, rotating stage erected in the middle of the racetrack. The announcer introduced them to the crowd.

"You all know our first driver," he began, and the crowd cheered. "He's the original funky monkey." The cheering intensified. "He's the king of kongs." More cheering, almost deafening. "Ladies and gents, boy-nanas and girls, I give you … *Chaaaamp the Chiiiimp!*"

Only the second introduction quieted the crowd. Otherwise, the audience might have kept on cheering for Champ. He was definitely their favorite.

"This year's challenger is a virtual unknown," the announcer informed the mute crowd. "He looks like a regular kid." Silence settled over the track. "He's, um, a boy." Crickets chirped. "I present ... Antwon!" Pins dropped.

Until Zoë belted out, *"MISTAKE!"*

"Make that Andrew," the announcer corrected. "Andrew the Average."

The crowd clapped politely but briefly. Nothing like the noise they made for Champ. The only genuine applause came from a troop of Traverse City fans.

"The first question goes to the challenger," the announcer said. "So, then, Antwon—er, Andrew—you're facing Champ the Chimp. How quickly do you expect to lose?"

Andrew cleared his throat and stood on tiptoe to reach the microphone. Even amplified, his voice sounded small.

"I don't," he replied.

"What!?" the announcer gasped in disbelief. Chuckles rolled through the crowd like a wave.

"I don't expect to lose," Andrew clarified. "I'm pretty good with wheels."

The announcer chuckled, too, joining most of the crowd. Few people expected Andrew to win.

"Well, Antwon's got spirit," said the announcer. "Good for him. Let's turn to Champ now." Applause erupted again, and the announcer had to shout to be heard. "Champ, tell us. What do you think of your hopeless opponent?"

The monkey rushed forward, snatched the microphone stand, and climbed up its length. From his perch, he surveyed the crowd and slowly raised his arms.

The crowd held its breath, waiting.

Champ flashed a double thumbs-up. He liked Andrew! Who would have guessed?

"Manners," Zoë nodded in approval. She appreciated Champ's seeming good sportsmanship. Unfortunately, she might have spoken too soon.

The spike on Champ's helmet flashed with energy. The monkey squished up his face, and shook his head. His thumbs-up melted into thumbs-down.

No, Champ didn't like Andrew. Not at all.

Now the monkey pointed at Andrew and waved his other hand beneath an armpit.

"Andrew stinks," the gesture said.

After the crowd caught on and laughed, Champ pointed at Andrew's truck, *Crime Crusher*. He slammed a fist onto an open palm.

Translation: "Champ crush!"

The crowd went wild. This was what they wanted. A feud. A duel. Two competitors engaged in battle like two knights of old jousting in armored vehicles. The clash between them would be epic.

Monkey vs. Man.

Boy vs. Banana.

Champ the Chimp had issued a challenge!

CHAPTER 8:
THE FINALS

Andrew clutched the steering wheel of *Crime Crusher* so hard his knuckles turned white. His face tightened in an involuntary scowl.

"You look tense," Abigail noticed. "Try to relax. Take a deep breath."

"Massage?" Zoë offered, flexing her short but very strong fingers.

Andrew blinked at his sisters, seeming to wake from a dream. "Huh? What?" When his eyes came into focus, he spoke slowly. "No. No, I'll be okay."

"You'd better be," Abigail said. "The race is about to start. It's an obstacle course."

Make that <u>the</u> Race. Capital *R*, underline *the*. Andrew had participated in dozens of races before. He'd won dozens of first-place trophies. But none of the races had been like this. Not against world champions. Not against Champ the Chimp.

"Just start already," he muttered to himself. Sitting still on wheels seemed like such a waste to him. There were roads to roam, trails to travel, expressways to explore, and boulevards to burn rubber. Andrew could roll on and on, and wished he were rolling right now.

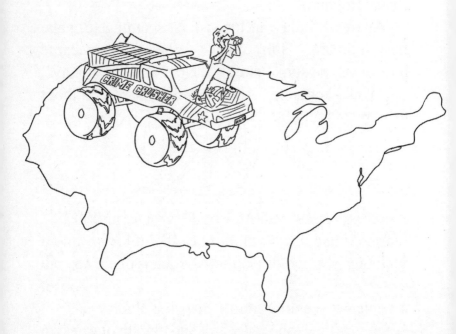

Lost in thought, Andrew almost missed the race's start. *Bang!* The shortest pause passed before his sisters shouted.

"Go!"

"Move!"

Andrew hit the gas.

He and Champ tore out of their starting positions. Exhaust fumes and dirt heaved into the air. The squeal of their tires filled the spaces in between.

First up in the obstacle course, the Monster Moguls. A series of bumps and jumps like a sea serpent's humps. Any average driver would take some lumps. Good thing Champ and Andrew weren't chumps!

Vroom! They went up. *Whoosh!* They flew. *Wham!* They landed, ready to do it again.

Stage two of the race consisted of the Slalom Slip. Andrew and Champ had to slither back and forth through rows of barrels. Yet neither of them was a snake! All the while, they were blasted by ski resort snow machines. Doubly dangerous this time of year.

Up next, the Jalopy Jam. A perilous pile of junk cars and trucks formed an ornery obstacle course. Champ and Andrew were allowed to drive only one way: over. Not under, around, or through the mound.

To the crowd's amazement, the drivers entered the last stage tied. What a race! The final challenge, Homestretch Highway, would determine a winner.

Andrew inched into the lead, pulling away. He grinned. He was going to win! The finish line rushed into view.

Boom!

Without warning, his right rear tire blew. A flat! *Crime Crusher* skidded out of control.

"Nooo!" Andrew cried, slamming on the brakes. So close! So far! So second place.

An instant later, Champ crossed the finish line. The victory flag dropped behind him and the race ended.

Champ the Chimp had won!

CHAPTER 9:
AND THE WINNER IS?

"Congratulations, Champ!" the announcer cheered over the P.A. system. "You win again! We all knew you could do it!" He sounded very pleased with the result of the race.

So, too, did much of the crowd at first. Some applauded the monkey. Some took his picture. Some made monkey noises and tossed bananas into the air like confetti. One proud family even hoisted their baby above their heads and shouted, "His name is Champ! We named him after you!"

What a scene! Almost everyone was celebrating. Hands clapped, feet slapped, voices shouted and screamed. Which is why it took Zoë several minutes to get their attention. Finally she flew up to the giant replay screen that hung above the racetrack. She pointed at it and sucked in a huge breath.

"MOVIE!" she bellowed the way only a superbaby can. That is to say, *very* loudly.

The crowd gasped and held its breath. Impossible! Unreal! The video on the screen couldn't be true. But it was. It really was. The video played again and again. No one at the racetrack could deny it.

The video clearly showed Champ firing banana darts at Andrew's truck during the race. That was what had caused *Crime Crusher's* flat tire. That was why Andrew had lost.

Champ the Chimp had cheated. Champ was a chump after all.

Now the crowd booed and hissed. A few people threw their bananas at Champ. They monkey screeched, dropped the winner's trophy, and darted under his truck for safety.

The announcer spoke up quickly, hoping to calm the crowd. "Judges! Let's hear from the judges. Did Champ the Chimp cheat? Should he be disqualified?"

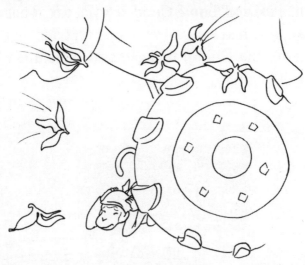

The first judge, Paula Doodle, was once famous for something. She rapidly sketched her decision on a large drawing pad. The other judges were afraid to let her speak. Don't even mention her singing! When she finished, she displayed her sketch for everyone to see.

It depicted Champ's face in a crossed-out circle. Who ya gonna call? Champbusters!

Paula Doodle had cast her vote against Champ. Guilty!

Simon Cowl, the second judge, wore a heavy black robe and hood. He looked like the emperor from Star Wars and was about as friendly. Dark garments completely hid his face.

The judge slowly raised an arm. A pale hand appeared from the loose sleeve. His thumb extended and his wrist rotated.

Thumbs-down! Not guilty. The vote was tied one-to-one. Champ hadn't been disqualified yet.

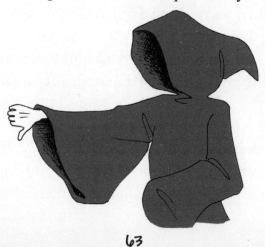

The third and final judge, Jackson Randall, petted the pink poodle perched on his lap. "What do you think, dawg?" he asked the poodle.

The poodle said nothing, so the judge looked to Champ. "What about you, dawg?"

Champ shrugged but also said nothing. That left Andrew. The judge turned to him. "And you, dawg?"

Andrew considered for a moment. "Cheaters shouldn't win," he said simply.

Judge Randall stared at him blankly.

"Bad dogs don't deserve treats," Andrew said, trying to speak the judge's language.

Now the judge smiled. He understood! "Well, alright, dawg!" he said. "You win!"

The crowd gasped and the announcer cleared his throat. "Attention, race fans. The judges have spoken." He didn't sound happy about it either. "In a stunning vote, Champ the Chimp has been disqualified. That means Antwon wins."

"Andrew," a second voice corrected.

"Andrew," the announcer repeated. "Andrew the Average wins. *Ho-hum.*"

Fans and family suddenly surrounded Andrew. They hoisted him onto their shoulders and stuffed a shining, golden trophy into his hands. Everyone smiled. Everyone cheered.

Everyone except for Champ the Chimp. He slouched off to the side alone, his helmet spike blazing an angry red.

CHAPTER 10:
GOING BANANAS

"Great job, little brother," Abigail congratulated her twin.

Andrew ignored the jab about his age. He had just won Michigan Monster Truck Mayhem. Almost nothing could spoil his good mood.

Not Mom, who hugged him tighter than a bear and cried, "My baby didn't hurt himself!"

Not Dad, who wiped tears from his eyes and whispered, "You're becoming a man."

And not Baby Zoë, who slapped Andrew on the back so hard that he fell down.

In fact, the only person who could ruin Andrew's mood wasn't a person. It was a monkey, *the* monkey. Champ the Chimp.

Unnoticed by everyone, Champ had crept back to his truck. He had climbed into the driver's seat and started the engine. Now he rudely blasted the horn.

Hooonnnkkk!

Which could mean only one thing. *Get out of the way!* Champ was about to steamroll everything and *everyone* in his path.

As soon as Champ let up on the horn, he slammed down the gas pedal. *Monkey Business* squealed into motion.

So did everyone on the racetrack. Frightened fans dashed fro and to, parting like curtains on a stage. Some scooped up children. Others lost their hats or dropped souvenirs. All that mattered was scrambling to safety.

Champ tore through the channel between them. His helmet spike pulsed and his lips curled into a snarl. No obstacle slowed him. Not even the racetrack's outer wall. *BOOM!*

"He's gone crazy!"

"Move it, Kid Roll! Catch that monkey!"

Surprisingly, it was the two gorilla bodyguards yelling at Andrew. The pair beat their hairy chests with their fists, looking terrified and terrifying at the same time.

"Catch him!"

"Hurry!"

Andrew looked to his parents for confirmation. He wouldn't take orders from the apes no matter how much noise they made.

"Go get him!" Mom mandated.

"Do your thing!" Dad declared.

Both shouted as loudly and as desperately as the gorillas. Andrew wondered if they, too, would pound on their chests.

He didn't wait to find out. The race had ended.
The fun was over. Now a mad monkey monster
trucker was on a rampage. Stopping Champ would
require superhero heroics, A^{2}Z style.

"Abigail, Zoë—let's roll!" Andrew called.

It was time to put a clamp on Champ.

CHAPTER 11:
MONKEY BUSINESS

Champ broke numerous laws as he sped away from the racetrack. He exceeded the speed limit. He passed on a double yellow. He failed to yield and use turn signals. Worst of all, he ate fast food and texted while driving—at the same time!

Naturally the heroes expected the worst when he veered into Grand Valley State University in Allendale, Michigan. Champ didn't disappoint. The monkey roared wildly through the streets, terrorizing everyone on campus. He finished his tour by bulldozing ten-story Cook Carillon Clock Tower.

Only Andrew's acrobatics saved the startled students. He bravely borrowed a bike and cycled them to safety. Class dismissed! Or was it class just missed?

The rescue, however, enabled Champ to escape. Helmet spike glowing like molten metal, the monkey turned his truck east. Soon he growled into Grand Rapids, Michigan, bashing bridges in a slap wheelie assault.

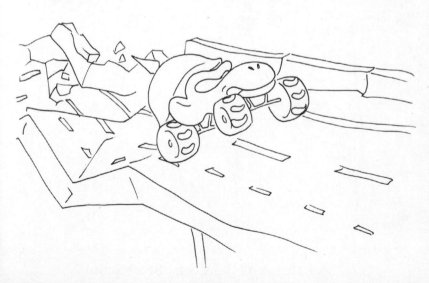

As the city's bridges cracked and crumbled, the vehicles on them started to tumble. Trucks toppled down jagged edges. Cars careened off broken ledges.

Their only hope? Abigail. She raced to the rescue like a combat medic in battle. Her medicine pouch was a duffle bag full of every kind of sports equipment. Thanks to her superpower, the bag never weighed too much to carry.

From it she scooped several bungee cords—perfect for extreme sports and more extreme rescues. Like an expert wrangler at a rodeo, she lassoed the veering vehicles before they crashed. Practice makes perfect.*

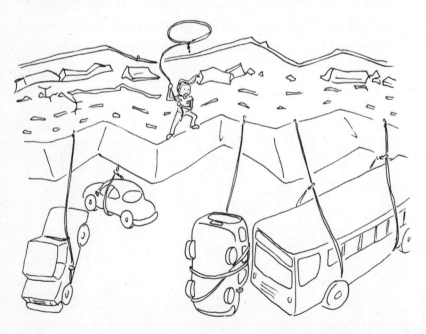

*See Heroes A²Z #3: Cherry Bomb Squad

Of course the battered bridges didn't slow Champ. He darted into downtown Grand Rapids, his ride rumbling like a demolition crew. The vibrations from his vehicle shook buildings and shattered glass. People started to fall from broken windows high above.

Which kept Zoë very busy and allowed Champ to slip away again.

Zip to the right! Zoë caught a custodian.

Zip to the left! Zoë seized a scientist.

Zip to the pavement! Zoë plucked a policeman out of midair.

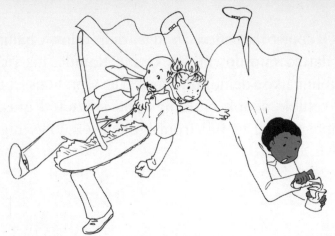

After Zoë set everyone down safely, she and her siblings regrouped. Champ had sped east again, escaping to the highway. From there, he could go almost anywhere.

"Midland?" Zoë guessed, naming another city in the state at random.

Her sister shrugged. "Maybe," Abigail said. "But it's hard to say. It's not like Champ is leaving breadcrumbs for us to follow."

Andrew snapped his fingers. "Breadcrumbs, that's it! Remember the clock tower," he said. Thinking this was a question, his sisters nodded.

"And the bridges," Andrew continued. More nods from the girls.

"And the earthquake downtown." Another pair of nods but also a confused look from Abigail.

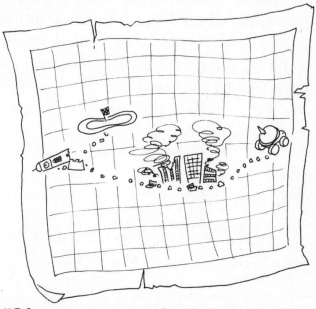

"Of course we remember," she said. "This stuff just happened."

"Exactly!" Andrew smiled. "Champ destroys stuff wherever he goes. It just happens. So to find him, we just have to follow the trail."

Zoë's eyes widened in understanding. "Map!" she cried. Champ *had* left breadcrumbs to follow. He'd left directions of destruction.

CHAPTER 12:
ROADBLOCK

As Andrew had predicted, the heroes easily followed Champ's trail. Overturned cars and mangled street signs littered the freeway. Black skid marks crisscrossed lanes, medians, exits, and on-ramps.

Everything along the road told the same story. Champ the Champ had been here.

Zoë's superhero sight spotted something in the distance first. A silver mass glinted on the horizon.

"Metal?" she wondered, squinting into the glare.

Good guess. Because as the heroes approached, the silver shape became clear. It was a roadblock stretched across every lane of the highway. Unlike roadblocks the heroes had seen before, this didn't involve the police.* This roadblock was composed entirely of angry-looking monkey monster trucks.

*See Heroes A²Z #12: Lost Puppy Love

The heroes quickly hit the brakes, stopping in the middle of the road.

"What's going on?" Abigail shouted at the trucks. "Where's Champ?"

Arms folded across his chest, the monkey stepped into view from behind the roadblock. Two gorilla bodyguards joined him, one to his left and one to his right.

"Great!" Andrew said to the gorillas. "You caught him already."

"Manacles?" Zoë asked, suggesting that Champ should be wearing handcuffs.

The gorilla on the left laughed, showing sharp teeth. "Clueless humans. We didn't catch Champ. He came to us."

Abigail shook her head. "That was lucky," she said. "Because he went crazy after losing the race. He was trying to escape."

"Wrong," the second gorilla grinned. "Champ works for us. He obeys our commands. Watch."

The first gorilla raised its arm and spoke into a watch-shaped device on its wrist. "Champ, capture these kids and feed them to the trucks."

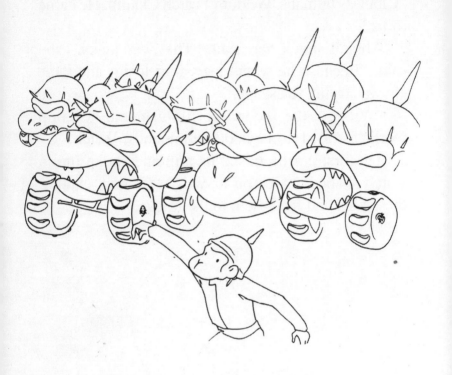

Champ jerked suddenly as if stuck by a pin. His eyes widened and the spike on his helmet pulsed. Stiff as a robot, he waved at the row of monster trucks, beckoning them to move.

The trucks' engines roared to life. Their headlights flared. Their hoods opened and closed repeatedly, snapping like the mouths of hungry crocodiles.

Outnumbered and outflanked, the heroes prepared for the worst.

CHAPTER 13: CHOMP!

As the mean monster trucks advanced, so did Andrew. He tucked his chin against his chest and sprinted straight for their line. It was muscle vs. motor in the bravest game of chicken ever.

Or the craziest!

"What are you doing?" Abigail called after him.

"Marbles!" Zoë shrieked, thinking her brother had lost his and gone mad. Those trucks wanted to swallow Andrew. He should be running in the opposite direction.

Andrew didn't listen and he didn't slow. He raced harder. Arms pumping, he leaned forward and dropped into a roll.

"Mashed!" Zoë cried. Marbles or not, Andrew was about to be pulverized like a potato.

Unless he jumped.

Which he did.

Using the momentum from his roll, Andrew leaped into the air. Rolling Kid Roll was a flying soul. Up, up he soared until Andrew scored his goal.

Thunk! He landed safely on the roof of the lead monster truck.

From the truck's roof, Andrew unleashed his superpower. The monster truck had wheels, so Andrew could ride it. Even if the truck had other plans.

Andrew leaned right, shifting his weight. Tires squealing in protest, the truck did the same. It veered sharply right and headed straight into the driver's side door of the nearest truck.

Crash! Both vehicles would be going nowhere but the junkyard now.

Zoë and Abigail cheered. Andrew hadn't lost his marbles, lost his mind, or gone mad. He was a hero! Moreover, Zoë wanted to help him.

"Matador!" she exclaimed, flying into the fray and removing her cape—her *red* cape, which she brandished like a bullfighter.

The nearest truck focused its blazing headlights on her. Its engine revved and roared, and the angry vehicle changed direction. Now it zoomed at Zoë.

Bravely, the little hero held her ground. She snapped her cape in challenge. Come and get me if you can!

Whoosh! It couldn't.

Just before the terrible truck steamrolled her, Zoë zipped into flight. She slipped over the vehicle without so much as a clip.

"Miss!" she taunted from the air.

The truck wasn't so lucky. *Crash!* It slammed head-on into another vehicle. Two more trucks headed for the heap.

Inspired by her siblings, Abigail dug into her duffle bag. She couldn't let Andrew and Zoë have all the fun! She needed a piece of sports equipment that could terminate a truck in its tracks.

Fishing pole? Too flimsy. Water skis? No help on land. Catcher's mitt? Get serious! Finally she nabbed a bowling ball from the bag. Perfect for the job.

The ball was perfect, yes, but also perfectly late. Abigail pivoted, preparing to strike. That's when she spotted the truck approaching behind her. Its hood yawned fully open. Its bumper nudged her knees. One second she was standing. The next she tumbled into the truck.

Chomp! The hood slammed shut, trapping Abigail in darkness.

Zoë and Andrew screamed. So much for having fun! Their sister had been swallowed and the remaining trucks surrounded them.

"Multitude!" she marveled. The trucks were too numerous to count. No matter how many she and Andrew destroyed, more took their place.

Chomp! A hood closed over Andrew, gulping him gluttonously. *Chomp!* Another snatched his sister.

Locked in the dark, the heroes could only wonder where the trucks would take them next.

CHAPTER 14:
HUMAN ZOO

The heroes hurtled down the highway. They rode separately. They rode in darkness. They rode locked under the hoods of monkey monster trucks.

None of them knew how long they rode. Or for how many miles. Or in which direction. When the trucks finally stopped, their hoods popped open. They spit the heroes out like old gum. Daylight stung the heroes' eyes.

"Where are we?" Abigail muttered, squinting at a sign overhead. The letters on the sign came slowly into focus. They read: POTTER PARK ZOO.

Potter Park Zoo was in Lansing, the capital of Michigan. The zoo usually featured over 150 species of animals. Today it had completely changed.

Most of its animals were gone. The eagles had escaped, the leopards had left, the skunks had skedaddled, and the hippos had high-tailed it. Only apes and monkeys remained. But they were not in cages or exhibits anymore. They patrolled the paths and walkways like uniformed police. Keys and clubs dangled from their belts.

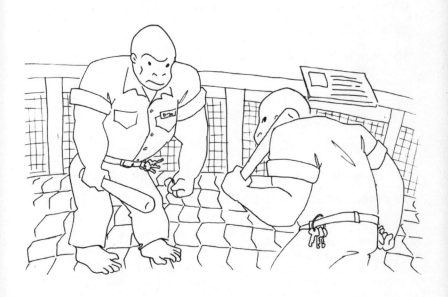

Humans now occupied the cages and exhibits. In one, gaggles of grandparents gathered in groups, gossiping about their growing grandkids.

In another, bands of babies bawled and burbled beneath the bars of backyard swing sets.

In a third, teams of teens talked, texted, and tweeted, totally transfixed by today's technology.

The heroes were given no time to investigate or to free the caged people. They were captives themselves! Gorillas grabbed their shoulders and dragged the heroes through the zoo.

"Put us down!" Abigail demanded.

"Stop right here!" Andrew commanded.

The gorillas ignored their orders. They did not stop or release the heroes until they reached a special cage in a faraway corner of the zoo. Then they heaved the heroes into the cage and slammed the door shut.

Abigail, Andrew, and Baby Zoë were prisoners in a human zoo!

CHAPTER 15: CAGED

The heroes' cage wasn't square or enclosed by bars. It was dome-shaped, clear, and made of one solid piece like an upside-down bowl. But what that piece was, the heroes didn't know. Maybe plastic, maybe glass, maybe both or neither.

What they knew was that they couldn't break the barrier. They punched, kicked, rolled, and rammed. Zoë even fired her eye lasers at it. No effect. Nothing the heroes tried damaged the dome. It remained unharmed and unbreakable.

Zoë collapsed into a crib in the cage. "Miserable," she whimpered, grasping the wooden bars in her fists. She felt like a prisoner. Might as well look like one.

The baby crib wasn't the only furnishing in the dome. A wooden half-pipe for skateboarding occupied the far end. Andrew scaled its ladder and sat glumly with his legs dangling over the ledge. For once, he didn't feel like breaking out his board.

Between the crib and half-pipe stood a tetherball pole, complete with rope and ball. Abigail glanced at it and frowned.

"These things were put here for us," she said. "Like tire swings for monkeys and slides for penguins. They're supposed to entertain us."

"Yeah," Andrew agreed. "While we entertain our audience. Look."

He half-heartedly pointed to the front of the dome. Wearing a soldier's uniform and his spiked helmet, Champ stood outside the cage watching the heroes. He mimicked Andrew's gesture by raising his arm and pointing at the boy.

"Leave us alone!" Abigail snapped at Champ. "You already captured us! Isn't that enough?" She made an irritated motion with her arms and hands, trying to shoo the monkey away.

Champ didn't obey. He grinned and repeated Abigail's gesture instead, waving his arms wildly. He seemed to be enjoying himself. He was playing.

An idea forming in her mind, Zoë floated out of the crib. She slowly turned her head from Andrew to Champ, then from Abigail to Champ. Without delay, the monkey imitated her. He looked at Andrew and then Zoë, at Abigail and back to Zoë.

The baby hero nodded confidently. "Mirror," she told her siblings. Champ was copying everything she and her siblings did. He was mirroring them.

Abigail gasped in understanding and dipped into her duffle bag.

"I get it!" she announced. "It's monkey see, monkey do. Champ is mimicking us."

Andrew hopped down from the half-pipe. "So let's pretend we're opening doors," he suggested. "Maybe Champ will open ours."

"I've got a better plan," Abigail countered. "Here it is!" She pulled a football helmet from the bag and jammed it on her head. Then she stood up, faced Champ, and ran.

"Here goes!" she shouted.

Her siblings could only watch and wonder. Was Abigail going to ram the cage's wall with her head?

CHAPTER 16:
MONKEY SEE, MONKEY DO

Abigail didn't run into the wall of the cage. She and her siblings had tried that already. Not even with a football helmet on her head would she try that again.

Instead she stopped inches from the wall, directly in front of Champ. On the other side, the monkey stared at her curiously. Abigail stared back. Slowly she raised her right foot. Champ raised his left in imitation. Monkey see, monkey do in mirror image. Next, Abigail raised her left arm. Champ mirror-copied her again and smiled. He really liked this game!

"Are you trying to teach him the hokey pokey?" Andrew asked.

Abigail, meanwhile, had lowered her leg. "Now for the challenge," she whispered. She placed her palms flat against the sides of her head. As she'd hoped, Champ mimicked the move. He placed his arms against his head. Then ever so slowly, Abigail lifted the football helmet from her head.

Champ froze and a look of concentration tightened his face. His smile vanished. He was struggling inside. Removing the helmet was forbidden. The gorillas had told him so. But monkey see, monkey do required him to imitate Abigail.

Breathless seconds passed. No one blinked but they all started to sweat.

Finally the monkey twitched. His fingers flexed. As a smile stretched his lips, he pulled the spiked helmet from his head.

"Miraculous!" Zoë squealed. Andrew and Abigail high-fived. Champ the Chimp was free!

The sibling celebration lasted only seconds. Champ quickly interrupted by flailing his arms. He also stomped his feet and screeched as if someone had pulled off his tail.

"Careful!" Abigail advised. "He's going ape."

"Bananas!" Andrew agreed.

But Zoë shook her head. Champ wasn't going crazy. He was ashamed of himself and of the bad things he had done. The helmet had turned him into a villain! Now that he had removed it, he was a nice, friendly monkey again.

"Mortified," Zoë explained. Champ was sorry for the crimes he had committed. He dropped to his backside and clutched his head in his hands.

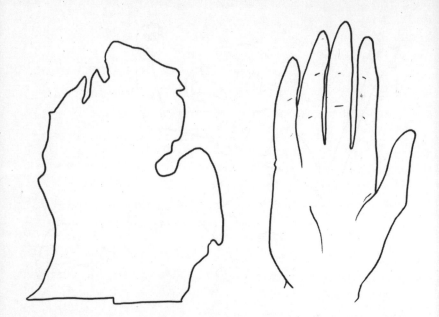

Now it was Abigail's turn to imitate Champ. She sat cross-legged in front of the dome and looked into his eyes.

"It's okay, Champ," she said soothingly. "We can fix what was broken. We just have to get out of here and find those gorillas. They're the ones responsible for everything."

The monkey raised his head and met Abigail's gaze. The smile returned to his face.

"Do you know where to find them?" Abigail asked.

Champ nodded and pointed at his right palm.

"Michigan," Zoë said. Champ was using his hand as a map. Michigan's Lower Peninsula was called the mitten for good reason. It looked like one!

"He's pointing at Flint," Andrew said, naming a city in mid-Michigan. "That must be where the gorillas are."

Champ's smile broadened and he nodded. Flint, Michigan, was it. He then unlocked the cage door, helped the heroes out, and sneaked them to the parking lot. Champ's truck, *Monkey Business,* sat unguarded in the lot.

Moving fast, Andrew snatched the keys from Champ's belt. "Who gets to drive?" he asked with a grin.

Zoë snatched the keys from him just as quickly. "Me!" she teased.

In the end, Champ drove while Abigail, Andrew, and Zoë ducked in the passenger seat. Every other vehicle on the road was driven by a monkey or ape. The heroes would have been noticed.

About an hour later Champ eased *Monkey Business* to a stop and turned off the motor. The heroes peeked over the dashboard at a massive brick building. Monster trucks rolled from an open garage door like marching soldiers. Atop the building stood a broad sign that read, "MONKEY MOTORS."

In a junkyard to the side of the building sat *Crime Crusher,* abandoned and alone.

CHAPTER 17:
MONKEY MOTORS

Yelling like Vikings, Champ and the heroes charged into Monkey Motors. They briefly considered sneaking inside, but the factory didn't have any open windows. It didn't have a secret back entrance either.*
The front doors were the only way in.

So the heroes and their monkey friend ran straight inside, making as much noise as they could. Abigail smacked two aluminum baseball bats together over her head. Andrew squealed the wheels on his skateboard. Zoë and Champ screeched like angry monkeys. Guess who was the loudest?

*See Heroes A²Z #8: Holiday Holdup

Monkeys filled the factory. They dangled from the rafters. They swarmed over half-built monster trucks. They drove forklifts, clutched tools, and wore greasy jumpsuits.

Zoë identified them easily. "Mechanics," she said. The monkeys were responsible for building new monster trucks.

The monkeys also seemed glad to see the heroes.
Many of them waved in greeting. Some of them
clapped and hopped from foot to foot. A few twirled
excitedly in place.

"Is this a monster truck factory or a dance party?"
Andrew murmured.

"Macarena?" Zoë asked, wondering the same
thing.

The monkeys weren't dancing, of course. They
were distracting the heroes. While most of them
performed, one monkey secretly triggered a silent
alarm. Doing so sent instructions to the monster trucks
outside.

When the trucks received the signal, they literally changed gears. Motors roaring, they broke from their orderly lines and sped across the parking lot in different directions.

"Mobilizing," Zoë said. The monster trucks seemed to be fleeing. Were they afraid? In a panic?

CRASH! Maybe both. Because without a honk or the squeal of brakes, one truck suddenly swerved into another. *CRASH!* Then a second did the same. *CRASH!* Followed by a third.

"O!" Abigail began.

"M!" Zoë continued.

"G!" Andrew ended.

Like cars in a demolition derby, the monster trucks were destroying themselves. Why else would they be running into each other on purpose?

One word, and Zoë said it. "Monstrosity," she announced, pointing outside.

The monster trucks weren't destroying themselves. Quite the opposite, in fact. The trucks were joining forces. They were growing. Like Lego bricks, the trucks were fitting together and building something new.

Something big.

Something dangerous.

"Is it too late to go back to the zoo?" Andrew whispered.

Eyes wide, Abigail nodded. "I think so. I doubt that thing will give us a ride."

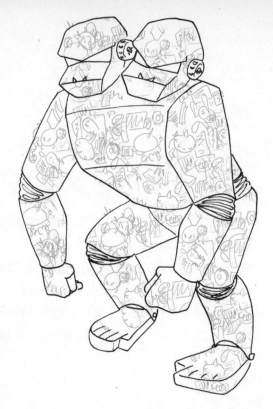

The crashing and smashing monster trucks had a plan and purpose. With every crash, they joined more snugly together. With every smash, they grew larger.

As the heroes watched, a giant metal gorilla formed in the parking lot of Monkey Motors. Call it Ape-ocalypse—part ape and part apocalypse, or the end of the world. It was not a troop of trucks anymore. It was one massive machine. Ape-ocalypse towered ten stories in the air. It had two arms, two legs, and two hands as big as the shovels of an earth mover.

Keeping with the *two's* theme, Ape-ocalypse also had two heads.

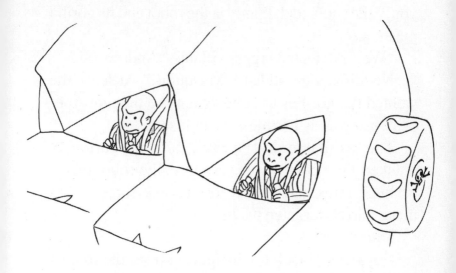

Ape-ocalypse reared back both heads and roared. The outburst sent clouds skidding across the sky.

"You have interfered long enough, humans!" declared the head on the left.

"Your end is here!" said the head on the right.

Staring up at Ape-ocalypse, the heroes cringed. They knew those voices. They had heard them today. The voices belonged to Champ's former gorilla bodyguards—the ones that had made him wear the hypnotizing helmet.

Moreover, the heroes could see the gorillas now that they knew where to look. The gorillas sat *inside* the robot's heads. Strapped to metal seats, they clutched control sticks like crane operators.

Abigail swallowed her fear. "We aren't afraid of you!" she shouted defiantly at the robot and its gorilla masters.

"We've defeated bigger villains," Andrew said.*

Nodding, Zoë added, "Mosquito!" At least she wanted the gorillas to believe that she thought Apeocalypse was as harmless as an insect.

The gorillas didn't speak , but they furiously cranked their controls. In response, the robot raised its huge arms and spread its massive fingers. Ten metal barrels targeted the heroes.

Squirt!

Geysers of black liquid spewed from the robot's fingertips. The dark downpour drenched the asphalt, the walls of Monkey Motors, and the heroes.

*See Heroes A²Z #10: Joey Down Under

114

Abigail slipped, Andrew tripped, and Baby Zoë took a dip. Not even Champ escaped the assault. In seconds, the four were covered in sticky slop from head to toe. They tried to run, but the slime was too slick. It was a special blend of oil and grease. All of them fell to the ground, as helpless as bugs in a web. Who were the insects now?

"Oily!" Abigail observed.

"Molasses!" Zoë moaned.

"Greasy!" Andrew grumbled.

Ape-ocalypse reared back its heads again. "You are finished, humans!" it howled. "This planet belongs to the apes!"

CHAPTER 18:
APE-OCALYPSE

Ape-ocalypse dwarfed Champ and the heroes. Its enormous ape-shaped shadow swallowed them and much of the parking lot.

"The time for humans is over," said the left head.

"*Your* time is over," said the right.

The words were clearly threatening, but Abigail wasn't listening. Even stuck in slippery slime, she refused to give up. The sporty superhero never quit.

"The final bell hasn't rung yet," she told the robot. "We aren't hanging up our gloves yet."

The final bell. Gloves. Put together, those reminded Abigail's athletic brain of boxing. And boxing gave her an idea for escape.

Before Ape-ocalypse fired more oil and grease, Abigail dug into her duffle bag. From it she pulled another kind of bag—a punching bag. Not a small speed bag, though. One of those body-sized bags that are shaped like cylinders and filled with sand.

With quick twists of her wrists, she untied the bag. Pounds of sand poured out in a rush.

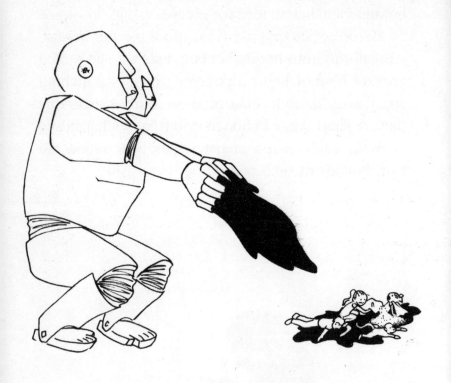

The robot watched Abigail with amusement. Both heads laughed. "Do you want a bigger mess?" one of them taunted. "Let us help."

Hydraulics whirring, the robot's hands came up again, preparing to fire another sloppy assault. As they slowly took aim, Champ and the heroes held their breath.

Still laughing, Ape-ocalypse attacked. *Squirt!*

Streams of slime streaked from the robot's fingertips. Some zeroed in on Zoë. Others attacked Andrew. One stream chugged at Champ, and three thrust at Abigail.

Astonishingly, all of them missed.

Why? Because the sand from Abigail's punching bag worked. The sand soaked up most of the slime that had kept them pinned in place. Now Champ and the heroes were free and moving fast. They scattered in four different directions.

Andrew raced for the junkyard, Champ for his truck. The girls, meanwhile, turned fearlessly to face Ape-ocalypse.

"Let's play a game," Abigail suggested, football in hand.

"Middle!" Zoë squealed, as in monkey-in-the-middle. Today's version would feature a two-headed metal ape in place of the monkey.

Abigail drew back her arm and threw like a pro. The football arced high into the air, whisked over Ape-ocalypse's head, and dropped into Zoë's hands.

"Touchdown!" Abigail cheered, and Zoë posed like a Heisman Trophy winner. She would be the first baby to win the college football award. The first since Abigail, anyway.

"Money!" Zoë exclaimed.

Between them, the robot angrily stomped its huge metal feet. "Fools!" it bellowed. "This is no time for games. Your species—"

Ape-ocalypse said nothing more. It couldn't. Andrew and Champ cut it off in mid-sentence. They also cut it off at the knees.

Crime Crusher and *Monkey Business* plowed into the robot at the same time. Andrew's truck struck the rear. Champ's flattened the front. It was a one-two punch in a double truck crunch.

BOOM!

Down. Went. Ape-ocalypse. The robot fell like a chopped tree. Nothing slowed its fall. Ape-ocalypse hit the ground, bounced, and went still.

Which was Abigail's cue to act. She pulled out her last bungee cord and rapidly looped one end around the robot's heads. The other end she tied to *Crime Crusher's* back bumper.

"Time to fly," she grinned at Andrew.

"Woot!" he cheered, eagerly pressing the special button on the dashboard of his truck. The eject button that made his truck fly like Zoë.

Next stop, Potter Park Zoo. Andrew lowered Ape-ocalypse and its gorilla drivers into their very own cage.

Later that day the heroes, their parents, Champ, and all the monster truck fans met at the racetrack. A real winner needed to be crowned. Afterward the heroes and monkey would fix the damage around Michigan.

In the meantime, Zoë raised her arms, a checkered flag in each hand. Champ and Andrew revved their engines. Then Zoë whipped her arms down and shouted one word: "Mush!"

The race was on … again!

Yet no matter who won the race, Andrew would always be Kid Roll. Like his sisters, he was a superhero. One race wouldn't change that. Nothing would. Not even an unexpected uprising by famous fictional characters in …

Book #14:
Nursery Rhyme Crime

Fighting Crime Before Bedtime

Also Available on the Kindle and Nook
See realheroesread.com for details

Connect with the Authors

Charlie:
charlie@realheroesread.com
facebook.com/charlesdavidclasman

David:
david@realheroesread.com
facebook.com/authordavidanthony

realheroesread.com

facebook.com/realheroesread
youtube.com/user/realheroesread
twitter.com/realheroesread

About the Illustrator
Lys Blakeslee

Lys graduated from Grand Valley State University in Michigan where she earned a degree in Illustration.

She has always loved to read, and devoted much of her childhood to devouring piles of books from the library.

She lives in Grand Rapids, Michigan (which fortunately hasn't seen any monkeys on the rampage too recently) with a bushy-tailed cat named Finny.

Thank you, Lys!